SHE ROSE

For the girl who knows who she is

and must fight to stay that way.

Kendra Tamika

Remember Her Publishing

She Rose

Published by Remember Her Publishing

ISBN: 979-8-9954705-6-4

LCCN: 2026909871

First Edition

Printed in the United States of America

She Rose is part of the Remember Her Girls Series published by Remember Her Publishing.

She Rose contains themes of first heartbreak, social media pressure, and neurodivergence that may be relevant for parent-child discussion. Recommended for ages 13 to 17.

For the girl who is standing at the beginning of something big.

You are not too much.
You are not too loud.
You are not too different.
You are not too anything.

You are exactly enough
in exactly the right amount
at exactly the right time.

She rose.
And so will you.

TABLE OF CONTENTS

A NOTE FROM THE AUTHOR

Nova was twelve when she remembered herself.

She is fifteen now.

And the world, as it tends to do, has gotten louder.

She Rose is for the girl who did the work of remembering and then discovered that remembering is not a one-time event. It is a daily practice. A daily choosing. A daily decision to show up as yourself in a world that has very specific and very loud opinions about who you should be instead.

It is harder at fifteen than it was at twelve. The stakes are higher. The voices are louder. The pressure comes from more directions at once.

But the girl who remembered herself at twelve has something that the girl who never forgot herself does not have.

She knows the way back.

And knowing the way back is everything.

With love,

Kendra Tamika

CHAPTER 1

The Girl Who Got In

I got in.
I am still not sure I believe it.
I got in on my manga.
The thing I almost stopped doing in sixth grade.
The thing I carried in my bag instead of in my hands for three months
because I was afraid of what people would think.
That thing.
That exact thing got me here.
I do not have a word for what that feels like.
I am going to draw it instead.

The acceptance letter had arrived on a Tuesday in March of eighth grade and Nova had been in her pink room, still pink, always pink, the pink had if anything deepened over the years as she leaned further into the things that were hers rather than away from them, working on a new sequence when her mother knocked on the door.

She knew immediately that something had happened.

Not because Reina said anything. Not because her expression was dramatic or her voice was elevated. It was the opposite of all of those things. Her mother's face had gone carefully neutral in the particular way it went carefully neutral when she was containing something large, when the thing she was feeling was too significant to let out casually in a doorway and needed the proper space to land.

She held out an envelope.

Nova set down her pencil.

She looked at the envelope for a moment before she took it. The return address in the upper left corner. The name printed in clean institutional font.

Westbrook Academy for the Arts. Office of Admissions.

She had applied in October. Assembled the portfolio over the course of three weeks, not just her recent work but a curated selection of everything she had made since sixth grade, the whole arc of her development as an artist, arranged with the deliberate intention of someone who understood that she was not just showing drawings but telling a story about herself. About her growth. About the specific and singular way her brain and her hands worked together to make things that could not have been made by anyone else.

At the center of the portfolio she had placed The Girl Who Remembered.

The full sequence. Eleven panels. The one that had started as a private processing of the worst semester of her young life and had become the thing that showed at the regional showcase and won second place and been seen by a judge who said you have a real gift like it was information rather than flattery.

She had submitted the portfolio and then done the thing she had learned to do with uncertain outcomes. She had put it in the part of her mind that held things she could not control and she had kept working. Kept drawing. Kept building the next thing without waiting for the verdict on the last one.

And now here was the envelope.

Her hands were not entirely steady when she opened it.

She unfolded the letter.

Dear Nova Cole, We are pleased to inform you that you have been accepted to Westbrook Academy for the Arts for the upcoming academic year. Your portfolio submission, specifically your sequential manga narrative The Girl Who Remembered, demonstrated exceptional technical skill, original storytelling, and a mature artistic voice that is rare in applicants of any age. We look forward to welcoming you to our community of young artists this fall.

She read it three times.

The first time her eyes moved across the words too quickly for them to fully land. The second time she let each sentence settle before she moved to the next. The third time she was not reading anymore. She was sitting with it. With the specific weight of a thing you have wanted for a long time finally arriving.

She put the letter down on her desk.

She looked at her sketchbook. At the sequence she had been working on when her mother knocked.

She looked at the stack of sketchbooks on her shelf. She counted them automatically. Fourteen. Fourteen sketchbooks filled since sixth grade. One thousand and something pages of drawings and journal entries and experiments and failures and the specific record of a girl teaching herself to see the world and then teaching herself to put what she saw onto paper.

The Girl Who Remembered had been in sketchbook number four.

The one she had made when she was twelve years old and the worst semester of her life had given her so much material she could not stop drawing even when she wanted to.

She thought about that version of herself. The sixth grade Nova who had left the sketchbook in her bag for three months. Who had held her stim in a hallway because someone used the word weird and she had let it shrink her for longer than she should have. Who had rushed through the morning ritual because the girl saying the words was not quite herself.

She thought about January of seventh grade. About carrying the sketchbook in her hand through the front doors of school. About the way that single decision had been the beginning of everything that followed.

The thing you almost stopped doing is the thing that opened the door.

She had written that in the margin of a sketchbook three years ago and she had meant it as a reminder to herself and she had not fully understood until this moment exactly how literally it would turn out to be true.

She picked up her pen.

She wrote in the margin of her current sketchbook, small and certain, just for herself:

I got in. On the manga. The thing I almost stopped doing. Never stop doing the thing. Never.

She heard her mother still standing in the doorway.

She turned around.

Reina was looking at her with the expression she had worn on the first day of sixth grade when Nova had walked out the door with her two bows and her unicorn backpack, the quiet certain pride of a woman watching someone she loves step fully into something they have earned.

"Well?" Reina said. As if she had not already read the answer in her daughter's face.

"I got in," Nova said.

Reina crossed the room.

She did not say anything. She opened her arms and Nova walked into them and they stood there in the pink room with the fourteen sketchbooks on the shelf and the acceptance letter on the desk.

"I knew," Reina said into the top of her locs. "I always knew."

"I didn't," Nova said honestly.

"I know," her mother said. "That's why I get to say I told you so."

Nova laughed. The real laugh. The one that started somewhere in her chest.

Westbrook Academy for the Arts occupied a converted building in the arts district of the city, forty-five minutes from the suburb where Nova had grown up. The building had been a warehouse once and still had the bones of it: high ceilings that rose thirty feet above the main studio space, exposed brick walls, enormous north-facing windows that ran along the entire length of the upper floor and poured a quality of light into the building that Nova had never experienced in any school before.

She stood in the entrance on the first day of freshman year and looked up.

The ceiling was at least thirty feet above her. The scale of it, the simple physical fact of that much space above her head, did something to her chest that she did not have a word for. Something that felt like expansion. Like the container of what was possible had just gotten significantly larger.

The walls were covered in student work.

Not the rotating display of the month's best submissions that she had seen at every other school she had attended. A permanent living gallery, pieces layered and pinned and hung at every height, some framed, some raw, some in progress. Paintings and photographs and textile works and digital prints and pencil studies and things that did not fit neatly into any category.

And in the corner near the entrance hallway, a series of manga panels.

Nova crossed the foyer without deciding to. Her feet moved toward them automatically. The panels were mounted in a clean grid, twelve of them, black and white, each one approximately eight by ten inches, telling a story she could not fully follow from the opening panels alone but that pulled her forward anyway with the particular quality that good sequential art always had.

The line work was exceptional.

Clean. Precise. Confident in the way that took years to develop.

Nova stood in front of those panels for a long time.

She felt two things simultaneously.

The first was the warmth of recognition. The specific warmth of finding your language in an unexpected place.

The second was something more complicated. A quiet assessment. The artist in her looking at those panels with clear honest eyes.

Those are good, she thought.

And then, without apology and without arrogance, simply as a fact: Mine are better.

She had not always been able to think that. There had been a time when she would have looked at someone else's excellent work and felt only the teeth of comparison. She knew what it felt like. She had lived inside that feeling.

This was different.

This was the clear-eyed confidence of someone who had done the work.

She looked around the room to see who might have made them.

Her eyes landed on a girl sitting at the opposite end of the worktable.

She was drawing already, head down, completely absorbed, her pencil moving with the fast instinctive energy of someone who drew the way other people breathed. Her hair was in long box braids pulled back with a paint-stained scrunchie. She had on a paint-stained oversized sweatshirt and the kind of focused expression that said the room could catch fire and she would finish this line first.

She looked up.

Their eyes met across the worktable.

The girl looked at Nova's sketchbook. Then at Nova. Then back at the sketchbook with an expression that was assessing rather than friendly.

Nova looked at the panels on the board. Then back at the girl.

The girl's eyes narrowed slightly. Not unkindly. Just recognizing something.

A rival.

Nova recognized it too.

She picked up her pencil.

She opened her sketchbook.

She started to draw.

Game on, she thought.

And almost smiled.

Her name is Jordan.
She made those panels in the entrance.
They really are good.
Mine are still better.
She would say the same thing about hers.
We have had exactly zero conversations today.
We have been watching each other across the worktable for six hours.
I think I am going to like this school.
Tomorrow I bring the good pencils.

Her father was in the pickup line when she came out at the end of the day.

She slid into the back seat with her sketchbook and her backpack and the particular exhaustion of a day that had been full in every sense: full of new information and new faces and new stimulation and the specific cognitive work of navigating an unfamiliar environment while also trying to be present to everything worth noticing in it.

Her foot started tapping against the floor mat before she had finished putting on her seatbelt.

Her dad looked at her in the rearview mirror.

"Well?"

Nova looked out the window at the arts district sliding past. At the murals on the buildings. At the people moving through the streets with the particular energy of people who had chosen to live in proximity to creative work because it mattered to them.

"The ceiling is thirty feet high," she said.

Her dad processed this. "Is that good?"

"It's the best thing I've ever seen in a school building."

He smiled in the rearview mirror. "What else?"

"There's a girl named Jordan who made manga panels and put them in the entrance. They're good." Nova paused. "I'm going to work harder than I have ever worked in my life."

Her dad was quiet for a moment. "Because of the ceiling or because of Jordan?"

"Both," Nova said.

He nodded like this was the exact right answer.

She Rose — Reflection

- ◆ What is the thing you almost stopped doing that might be the very thing that opens the next door for you?
- ◆ Nova felt two things at once when she saw Jordan's panels: recognition and honest assessment. Have you ever felt that same combination? What did you do with it?
- ◆ What does it feel like to walk into a space where you immediately know you belong? When was the last time you felt that?
- ◆ What would you write in the margin of your sketchbook today if you were being completely honest with yourself?

> *The thing that makes you different is not a liability. It is your qualification. It is the thing that opens doors. The sketchbook you almost left in your bag forever, the gift you almost traded for belonging, that is the thing that got you here. Never stop doing the thing.*

She Rose

She got in on the work she almost stopped making. Remember that every time you are tempted to put down the thing that is most specifically and completely yours.

CHAPTER 2

The Language of Art

There are students here who have been drawing longer than I have.

Students who have had formal training since they were five years old.

Students whose parents are artists.

I am aware of all of this.

I am not intimidated by any of it.

I am energized by it.

I think that is new.

I think that is growth.

I think I like who I am becoming.

The thing about arriving at a school for artists was that the ordinary rules of academic hierarchy did not apply in the ways Nova had come to expect them to.

At her middle school the social architecture had been relatively legible once you understood it. The popular students occupied specific tables and specific hallways and their status was maintained through a combination of social fluency and the careful management of who was included and who was not. The currency was belonging. The threat was exclusion.

At Westbrook the currency was different.

It was work.

Not grades, though grades existed and mattered. Not social fluency, though Westbrook students were generally more interesting to talk to than any group of teenagers she had previously encountered. The currency was the work itself. What you made. How you made it. What it said and how it said it and whether it had the specific quality that every student at Westbrook could recognize but not always articulate:

the quality of having been made by someone who was fully present in the making of it.

You could not fake that quality.

You either had it or you were working toward it.

And everyone was working toward it.

The first week at Westbrook established the rhythm of the place in ways that Nova filed away carefully.

The academic classes in the mornings, taught by teachers who had clearly been selected not just for subject expertise but for the ability to connect their subject to the creative life of their students. Her English teacher assigned Persepolis alongside Their Eyes Were Watching God and ran discussions that treated both as equally serious literary texts. Her history teacher opened the first class by projecting a painting and asking not what is this but what is this saying, and then how is it saying it.

Nova had never been in a history class that felt like this.

She wrote in her sketchbook that evening: School has always felt like a place where I had to leave part of myself outside. Here it feels like they want all of me inside. I am still figuring out what to do with that.

The studio time in the afternoons was something else entirely.

Three hours of dedicated creative work time, five days a week. The studio available to all students, organized loosely by medium but not rigidly so, the expectation being that serious artists understood how to manage their own time and did not require the constant direction of a teacher to tell them what to work on next.

Nova had been drawing independently for years. She understood how to manage her own creative time.

She had not understood until she experienced it inside an institution how different it felt to be given that time within a context of collective seriousness. To be in a room full of people who were all using their three hours with genuine focus. No one performing productivity for a teacher's observation. No one waiting to be told what to do. Just people working. People making things.

She had never been so productive in her life.

She had also never been so aware of how much she still had to learn.

The Advanced Sequential Art seminar met on Tuesday and Thursday afternoons in the smaller studio on the third floor.

Nova had been placed in it, an unusual placement for a freshman noted in her enrollment paperwork with a small asterisk and the notation portfolio exception, and she arrived on the first Tuesday with her sketchbook and her good pencils and the quiet internal awareness that she was about to be in a room with students who were older than her and had more experience than her.

It was going to require something from her that went beyond technical skill.

It was going to require her to be genuinely uncertain.

Not performed uncertainty. Not the false modesty of someone who knew they were good pretending otherwise. Actual uncertainty. The acknowledgment that the edges of her knowledge were visible from where she stood and that the work of this class was going to happen right there at those edges.

She had not always been good at that.

She was about to find out exactly how much better she had become.

Mr. Osei arrived at precisely two o'clock.

He was tall and moved with the deliberate unhurried quality of someone who had long since stopped performing urgency. His canvas jacket, the paint-stained one that Nova would come to understand was not a single jacket but simply the jacket, was open over a dark shirt. His sketchbook was under his arm. It was battered in the specific way that sketchbooks got battered when they were genuinely used, the spine repaired with electrical tape in at least three places, the cover worn soft at the corners.

He looked like a working artist.

Not a teacher who had once been an artist.

A working artist who also happened to teach.

He set his sketchbook on the table at the front of the room. He looked around at the eight students seated at the worktable with the calm assessing gaze of someone who was building an accurate picture of who was in the room.

His eyes stopped briefly on Nova.

Not longer than anyone else. Just briefly. A data point registered and filed.

He sat down.

He did not introduce himself. He did not explain the class. He did not distribute a syllabus or give the opening speech that teachers gave at the beginning of courses.

He said: "Show me what you're working on."

Silence.

Then, slowly, with the particular uncertainty of students who had not been given clear enough instructions to feel safe, people began opening sketchbooks and placing work on the table.

Nova opened her sketchbook to the sequence she was currently developing. Not The Girl Who Remembered. She had brought that to the portfolio review but she was not going to lead with old work in this room. The new sequence. The one whose story she was still discovering.

She placed it on the table.

Mr. Osei moved around the table slowly. He stopped at each student's work for a different amount of time. He was looking at each piece with the same focused quality. Taking what he needed from it.

He stopped at Nova's sketchbook.

He looked at it for a long time.

Longer than he had looked at anyone else's work.

Nova kept her expression neutral. Her foot tapped under the table. Her hands stayed still on top of it.

Mr. Osei turned back two pages. Then forward one. He was reading the sequence the way a reader read, not panel by panel in isolation but as a whole, following the visual grammar of it, understanding how each image related to the ones before and after it.

He straightened up.

He looked at Nova.

"How long have you been working on this one?"

"Three weeks," she said.

"How long have you been drawing?"

"Seriously? Since I was nine."

He nodded. Not with approval. Just with the registration of information.

"What's the story?"

"I'm still finding it," she said honestly. "I know the character. I know what she wants. I don't know yet what's going to stop her from getting it."

"Good," he said.

She had not expected that.

"Good?"

"You're in the right place in the process," he said. "Most students your age try to know the ending before they've earned it. They skip the uncertainty." He looked back at the sketchbook. "Your line work is strong. Your panel composition is sophisticated. Your sense of visual pacing is better than students two years ahead of you."

Nova waited.

She could hear the and coming.

"And," he said, "your work is too safe."

The room was quiet.

"Safe how?" she said.

He pointed to a panel, the one she was most satisfied with, a full-page spread that had taken her four drafts to get right. "This is excellent. You know it's excellent. You can see it on the page: the care, the control, the technical mastery. You made this excellent on purpose and it shows." He looked at her directly. "The most important work you will ever make will not feel excellent when you are making it. It will feel uncertain. Wrong. Like you don't know what you're doing." He tapped the table. "That's where your next level lives. On the other side of the certain."

Nova sat with that for a moment.

The room was still quiet around her.

"So what do I do?" she said.

"Make something you're not sure about," he said simply. "Something that scares you. Something where you don't know if it's working until it's done. Something where your technical skill is not enough to save you and you have to find something else to rely on." He straightened. "That something else is where your real voice is. Everything you've made so far has been preparation for finding it. Now go find it."

He moved on to the next student.

Nova sat with what he had said.

She turned to a fresh page in her sketchbook.

She wrote his words down because she knew she was going to need them on the days she could not hear them clearly.

Make something uncertain. The real voice is on the other side of the certain. The most important work feels wrong when you are making it.

She looked at the words.

She drew a small star next to the third one.

Then she picked up her pencil.

She started making something she was not sure about.

Mr. Osei said my work is too safe.
I have been thinking about that for three days.
Safe means staying inside what I already know how to do.
Safe means making the thing that will definitely work
instead of the thing that might not.
Safe means my ego is protecting itself at the expense of my growth.
I do not want to make safe work.
I did not come to this school to make safe work.
New rule: if I am comfortable I am not trying hard enough.
Starting now.
No exceptions.

She Rose — Reflection

- ◆ Where in your life are you making safe work? Where are you staying inside what you already know works because it is comfortable?
- ◆ What would happen if you made something you were not sure about, if you showed up fully without the protection of your own competence?
- ◆ What is the new rule you need to write in the margin of your own sketchbook today?
- ◆ Who is the Mr. Osei in your life, the person who tells you the truth about where you are holding back?

> *I am not here to be impressive. I am here to grow. Growth lives on the other side of comfort. I am willing to be uncertain. I am willing to be wrong. I am willing to make the work that scares me. That is where my real voice is. I am going to find it.*

She Rose

The most important work you will ever make will not feel excellent when you are making it. Make it anyway. Especially then. Especially when it feels wrong. That is when you are closest to the real thing.

CHAPTER 3

When They See You

I posted the uncertain work today.
Three panels.
The ones made following Mr. Osei's rule.
I pinned them to the board in the main hallway
before I could talk myself out of it.
My hands were shaking slightly when I did it.
Not from fear exactly.
From the specific vulnerability of showing something
that you are not sure about yet.
It is on the board now.
Whatever happens next happens next.
Post the uncertain work.
That is the new rule.

The student work board in the main hallway of Westbrook was a democratic space.

That was the word Mr. Osei used when he introduced it to the freshman class in the first week: democratic. Not curated. Not selected by faculty for quality or appropriateness. Democratic. Any student could pin anything to it at any time. Work in progress. Work in question. Work that was finished. Work that was barely started.

The only rule was honesty.

You could not put something on the board that was not actually yours, not in the sense of authorship but in the deeper sense. Not something you had made while performing for an audience. Not the safe version. The board was for real work. The work that had cost something to make.

Students knew the difference.

The board always knew the difference.

Nova had spent three weeks making uncertain work before she felt ready to post any of it.

Not because she was waiting for it to become certain. That would have defeated the entire purpose. She was waiting for something else. For the specific moment when she looked at what she had made and felt two things simultaneously: the genuine uncertainty about whether it was good and the genuine conviction that it was hers. That it had come from somewhere real in her and could not have been made by anyone else.

The three panels she eventually pinned to the board had been made in three separate sessions over the course of a week.

The first she had drawn with her non-dominant hand for the first thirty minutes before switching. Mr. Osei had suggested this as an exercise in disrupting technical habit, in getting past the part of the brain that already knew how to do the thing and reaching for the part that did not. The resulting line work had a quality she had never achieved with her dominant hand: a looseness, a searching quality, the visual record of a hand that was figuring something out as it went.

The second she had drawn in the dark. Ten minutes of complete darkness, her desk lamp off, her phone face down, and then she had turned the light on and looked at what her hands had made without her eyes. The shapes on the page were not random. They had the logic of her internal visual language even without the oversight of her vision to keep them controlled.

The third she had drawn without stopping. Not a time limit. She had drawn until the page was full, without lifting the pencil, without evaluating what was happening, without the micro-corrections she usually made every few seconds. The uninterrupted flow of it had produced something she did not have a name for. Not a panel in the traditional sense. The visual record of a thought moving through her neurodivergent brain at full speed.

She had looked at the three panels together on her desk for a long time.

Are these good? she had asked herself honestly.

She did not know.

That was the point.

She had pinned them to the board.

She was coming around the corner of the main hallway two days later when she saw someone standing at the board.

A boy. Tall. Natural hair. Paint on his hands, not fresh paint, the kind that lived in the creases of your palms when you painted enough. He was looking at her panels with the focused attention of someone who was actually seeing them rather than just passing by.

He did not know she was behind him.

She watched him for a moment.

He leaned closer to the third panel, the one she was most uncertain about, the one drawn in the dark that had turned out stranger than she expected. His head tilted slightly. He reached up and his finger hovered just over the surface, the respectful almost-touch of someone who knew better than to put their hands on someone else's work, tracing the line of something in the panel.

"Huh," he said quietly. To nobody. Just the panel and himself.

It was not a negative huh.

It was the huh of someone finding something they had not expected.

Nova cleared her throat.

He turned around.

He had warm brown eyes and the expression of someone who had just been caught doing something completely innocent and knew it was innocent but was still slightly embarrassed anyway.

"Sorry," he said. "Are these yours?"

"Yeah," Nova said.

He looked back at the panels. Then at her. Then at the panels again.

"The third one," he said. "How did you do the texture on the left side of the second panel?"

It was not the question she had expected. Not these are great or I like your style or any of the social things people said about art when they wanted to say something without saying much. It was a specific technical question from someone who understood enough to ask it.

"I drew it in the dark," she said.

He looked at her. "Seriously?"

"For the first ten minutes. Then I turned the light on."

He looked back at the panel. "That's why it has that quality. The lines don't know where they're going." He said it with admiration. "That's really smart."

"It was Mr. Osei's idea," Nova said. "Sort of. He told me to make something uncertain."

"Mr. Osei told me the same thing last year," the boy said. He looked at her properly now. "I'm Marcus. Sophomore. Photography and mixed media."

"Nova. Freshman. Sequential art."

"The manga panels upstairs are yours too," he said. It was not a question.

"Yeah."

"Those have been up since the first week. Everyone's been wondering who made them."

Nova had not known that. She felt something warm move through her chest.

"They're older work," she said. "I'm trying to move past them."

"Move past them?" He looked genuinely surprised. "Those panels are incredible."

"They're safe," Nova said. And then felt slightly strange for saying it. It was a private language, hers and Mr. Osei's. But Marcus nodded like he understood completely.

"Yeah," he said. "Mr. Osei will do that to you." A small smile. "In a good way."

They stood in the hallway by the student work board for twenty more minutes talking about art. About the specific challenge of sequential storytelling versus single image. About the difference between narrative time and visual time. About the moment in the creative process when you stopped thinking and started making and what it felt like when that happened.

Nova did not notice the time passing.

She only noticed when the bell rang and they both looked up simultaneously with the slightly startled expression of people returning from somewhere.

"I have to" they both said at exactly the same moment.

They both stopped.

Marcus laughed. It was a good laugh, unguarded and real.

"See you around Nova," he said.

"See you around Marcus," she said.

She walked to her next class with her foot tapping and her hands making their small pattern at her sides and a feeling in her chest that was new and warm and slightly terrifying in the best possible way.

She did not draw it.

But she thought about it all day.

He saw the panels before he saw me.
He asked a technical question.

He understood what I meant by safe.
He laughed like he meant it.
I do not know what this is.
I know what this might be.
I am going to draw something uncertain tomorrow.
I think that is related.
I think everything is related.

She Rose — Reflection

◆ When was the last time someone asked you a real question, one that proved they had been actually paying attention to who you specifically are?

◆ What is the difference between being admired and being seen? Which one have you experienced more?

◆ What would it mean to stop making posed work in your art, in your relationships, in the version of yourself you show the world, and start making captured work instead?

◆ What is the uncertain work you have been afraid to post? What would happen if you posted it?

> *I am worth seeing. Not the posed version of me. Not the managed version. Not the version I curate for other people's comfort. The real version. The uncertain working-it-out version. That version is worth seeing. The right people will want to see it. I will let them.*

She Rose

He saw the panels before he saw her. And when he saw the panels he saw her anyway. That is what honest work does. It shows you to the right people whether you are ready or not.

CHAPTER 4

The Comparison Trap

I did something tonight that I know better than to do.
I looked at Jordan's Instagram for forty-five minutes.
Not casually.
Not in passing.
Forty-five minutes.
Scrolling.
Counting.
Comparing.
I know exactly what I was doing.
I was doing it anyway.
That is the thing about the comparison trap.
Knowing it exists does not make you immune to it.
It just means you recognize the teeth
while they are already in you.

It started the way these things always started.

Innocuously. Without intention. The specific casual chain of events that led somewhere you had not meant to go, the way you could start by looking at one thing and end up somewhere completely different forty-five minutes later with no clear memory of the individual decisions that had gotten you there.

Nova had been on her phone after dinner.

Not looking for anything specific. Just the ambient scrolling that happened in the space between finishing work and going to sleep. Not producing anything, not consuming anything with full attention, just existing in the flow of it.

She had been on her own profile.

Looking at her last three posts with the half-present attention of someone reviewing their own work not for quality but for documentation. Making sure the record existed.

Four thousand and two hundred followers.

She had gained two hundred since the school year started. Slow and steady, the kind of growth that came from making real work and sharing it consistently.

She was fine with that.

She had been fine with that.

And then, in the suggested follows section, Jordan's profile appeared.

She had not searched for it.

She had not been looking for it.

It was just there.

She clicked on it.

Jordan's profile was, Nova had to be honest with herself even when honesty was uncomfortable, exceptional.

Not just the work itself. The whole presentation. The careful curation of an artistic identity that was specific and coherent and immediately recognizable as belonging to one particular person. The color palette of her grid was consistent. Her posts alternated between finished work and process content with a rhythm that felt intentional without feeling calculated.

She posted every day.

Sometimes twice.

Nova scrolled.

And scrolled.

And kept scrolling.

It was, objectively, a remarkable body of documentation.

And underneath that objective acknowledgment, something else was happening.

Something quieter.

Something with teeth.

She checked the follower count.

Eleven thousand, four hundred and twelve.

She went back to her own profile.

Four thousand and two hundred.

She went back to Jordan's.

Eleven thousand, four hundred and twelve.

She was aware, clearly, fully, that she was doing something that was not good for her. That the comparison she was making was not useful. That follower counts were not a measure of artistic value.

She knew all of that.

She kept scrolling anyway.

The thing about the comparison trap that nobody told you was that it did not feel like a trap from the inside.

From the inside it felt like research. It felt like staying informed. It felt like the reasonable and responsible act of a serious artist understanding the landscape of their field.

But the data it was gathering was poison.

Not because Jordan's work was not genuinely good. It was. Nova had respected it from the first time she saw the panels in the entrance hallway. That respect was real and it was not the problem.

The problem was what her brain was doing with the comparison.

The specific internal narrative that was constructing itself, quietly, without her full permission, in the background of her scrolling: about what the difference between four thousand and eleven thousand meant. About what it said about the relative quality of their work. About whether Nova was behind.

Whether she was simply not as good as she thought she was.

That was the trap.

Not the comparison itself. The story the comparison told.

She put the phone down.

She picked it up again.

She scrolled for ten more minutes.

Then she put it face down on her desk and did not touch it.

She tried to draw.

She opened her sketchbook to a fresh page and picked up her pencil and sat with the blank page for a long time.

Nothing came.

This had never happened to her before. Not in this specific way. She had had creative dry spells. Days when the work was harder than usual. That was normal.

This was different.

This was not resistance. This was silence. The specific creative silence that came not from exhaustion or from having nothing to say but from the particular way comparison had shut down the part of her brain that made things. The part that needed to be unselfconscious to function.

Comparison moved you outside yourself.

That was the real damage it did.

Not the hurt feelings. Not the self-doubt. Those were symptoms. The actual damage was the relocation: the way it took you out of your own interior world and placed you in a comparative external one where the only question was how you measured up.

And you could not make anything real from that position.

You could only measure.

She sat with the blank page for twenty more minutes.

She wrote in the margin, small and honest:

I spent 45 minutes on Jordan's Instagram. I got nothing done after that. The comparison trap is real and I walked right into it. My creative brain shut down. This is what it costs.

She looked at the words.

She thought about Mr. Osei's rule.

If I am comfortable I am not trying hard enough.

She thought about the new rule she had made for herself.

Post the uncertain work.

She thought about what Jordan's profile had actually shown her: not the follower count, not the comparative metrics, but the thing underneath all of it. The evidence of a person who showed up every single day and made something and put it into the world.

That was not a threat.

That was a model.

She opened Instagram again.

Not to scroll Jordan's profile. To open her own.

She photographed the panels.

She posted them without a caption.

Just the images. Just the work. The uncertain work she had made in the dark and with her non-dominant hand and without stopping.

She put her phone face down.

She picked up her pencil.

She started drawing.

Not carefully. Not with the managed quality of work made while monitoring the output. With the fast instinctive energy of someone who had relocated back into their own interior world and was making from that place.

The lines came.

The page filled.

The specific silence lifted the moment she stopped measuring and started making.

She drew for an hour.

When she looked up the room was dark except for her desk lamp and her phone was lit up with notifications she had not heard arriving and the drawing in front of her was alive in the way that only the drawings made without self-consciousness were alive.

She looked at it for a long time.

Then she wrote at the bottom of the page:

The antidote to comparison is not confidence. It is making. Get back inside the work. The work does not care how many followers anyone has. The work only cares if you are present. Be present. Always. That is the whole answer.

The uncertain work reached more people than the certain work.
Three hundred likes before I went to sleep.
A thousand by morning.
I am not going to make the mistake of thinking
that the numbers are the point.
The numbers are a signal.
The signal is: the honest work reaches people.
You cannot manufacture that.
You can only make the honest thing
and trust that the people who need it

will find their way to it.
That is always the answer.
For art.
For everything.

She Rose — Reflection

◆ Where in your life are you measuring yourself against someone else's metrics and letting the measurement tell a story about your worth?

◆ What does comparison cost you specifically? What shuts down when you go into comparison mode?

◆ What is the antidote for you? What gets you back inside your own truth when comparison has pulled you outside of it?

◆ What is the uncertain work you have been afraid to post because you were worried about how it compared to someone else's?

> *My journey is my journey. Someone else's progress is not my failure. Someone else's numbers are not my verdict. I come back to myself. I come back to the work. I make the honest thing. That is enough. That has always been enough. That will always be enough.*

She Rose

The antidote to comparison is not confidence. It is making. Every time. Get back inside the work. That is the whole instruction.

CHAPTER 5

The Boy With the Sketchbook

Marcus asked me to look at his work today.
Not casually.
Not in passing.
He came to find me specifically.
In the studio.
During open work period.
And said: I want to show you something.
With the specific directness of someone
who had decided to do a thing
and was doing it.
I followed him.
I did not know yet what I was walking into.
I know now.
I am going to need a new sketchbook page.
This feeling does not fit in the margins.

The thing about Westbrook that Nova had not anticipated was how much of the real education happened in the spaces between the scheduled things.

Not in the classrooms. Not in the studio during the designated three hours. In the hallways between periods. In the courtyard at lunch when the weather was still mild enough to be outside. In the darkroom at the end of the afternoon when the building was quieting down and the students who were serious enough to stay past the last bell were there because they had nowhere they needed to be more urgently than in the middle of their work.

She had been staying late.

Not every day. She had the commute to account for, the forty-five minutes each way that put a practical boundary on how long she could reasonably extend her time in the building. But three days a week she stayed through the late afternoon.

Marcus stayed late too.

She had noticed this without meaning to. The way you noticed the patterns of people who occupied the same spaces as you. The accumulation of presence. The repeated observation of someone in the same place at the same time until their being there became part of the expected landscape.

He was usually in the darkroom or the mixed media studio on the third floor. She was usually in the sequential art room one floor down. They passed each other in the hallways sometimes, a nod, an acknowledgment, occasionally a few words about whatever either of them was working on.

She looked forward to those hallway moments more than she had admitted to herself until now.

She was admitting it now.

He came to find her on a Tuesday.

Open work period. The main studio at full capacity. Nova was at her usual spot at the end of the long worktable by the north windows, working on the fifth panel of the new sequence with the focused unhurried attention she brought to work that was going well.

It was going well.

She was inside it, fully, completely, the peripheral world of the studio receding to a background hum while the world on the page became the foreground, when she felt rather than heard someone approach.

She looked up.

Marcus.

Camera bag over one shoulder. The particular expression she had come to associate with him: the direct warm focus that was not performing attentiveness but simply being attentive. And something else underneath it. Something she had not seen on his face before.

Uncertainty.

"I want to show you something," he said. "If you have a few minutes."

She put down her pencil.

"I have a few minutes," she said.

The photography darkroom was on the second floor in the east wing, a part of the building Nova had rarely had reason to visit.

The transition from the bright hallway to the red-lit interior took a moment to adjust to. Not darkness exactly. The red safe light created a quality of visibility that was complete but altered, the world rendered in the specific palette of the darkroom. Red and shadow and the chemical smell that was distinctive and not unpleasant, the smell of images being drawn out of light-sensitive paper, of moments being made permanent.

Prints hung to dry on lines strung across one section of the room.

She understood immediately why Marcus had chosen it.

"Close the door," he said.

She closed it behind her.

The hallway sounds disappeared.

She turned to look at the series.

Twenty photographs.

Black and white. Mounted on the wall in four rows of five, not randomly arranged but sequenced, the way a story was sequenced, each image in a specific relationship to the ones before and after it.

All portraits.

But not the kind she had expected. Not the dramatic lighting and posed compositions that photography students often defaulted to when they were learning to use their technical skills. These were captured moments. Unguarded. The specific unrepeatable instant of a person being most themselves without knowing anyone was watching.

A woman laughing, not posing for laughter, actually laughing, the specific physical expression of genuine amusement that could not be manufactured. An elderly man looking at something off-frame with an expression that contained entire decades of living. A child at a rain-wet window, her hand pressed against the glass.

Nova moved along the series slowly.

She was reading it the way she read sequential art: not each image in isolation but as a whole, the cumulative meaning of the sequence greater than any individual photograph. The story being told across all twenty images was not a narrative story. It was a thematic one. A study in the quality of attention. In what human beings looked like when they were fully absorbed in something outside themselves.

She reached the middle of the series.

And stopped.

The fourteenth photograph.

Her three uncertain panels. Pinned to the student work board in the main hallway. Shot from a slight angle so that the hallway stretched behind them in shallow focus. The north window light falling across the panels from the left, illuminating them in a way that made the line work visible in three dimensions.

He had made her panels look like they were breathing.

She looked at the photograph for a long time.

"You took this," she said.

"Yeah." He was standing slightly behind her and to the right. Close enough to see what she was looking at. Far enough to give her space to look.

"When?"

"The week after you posted them. They were still on the board." A pause. "The light was doing something specific that afternoon. I wanted to catch it before it changed."

Nova looked at the photograph.

At her panels inside his photograph. At the way his eye had found something in them that she had not seen when she made them, not the individual panels but the presence they created together.

"This is part of a series about attention," she said. It was not a question.

"Yes," he said.

"About what people look like when they are fully present in something outside themselves."

"Yes."

She turned to look at him.

"You put my work in a series about full presence."

He met her eyes directly. "Your panels have that quality. The uncertain ones especially. You can see it: the specific thing that happens when someone stops managing the output and just makes. It's visible in the work itself." He paused. "I wanted to document it."

Nova felt the words land.

Not just about the art.

The recognition she felt in that moment was specific and distinct from any recognition she had received before. Not the judge at the regional showcase. Not Mr. Osei. Not the thousand likes on her post.

This was someone who had looked at what she made and seen her inside it. Had recognized her, her specific presence, her specific way of being in the world, in the work itself and had considered it worth documenting.

Had put her in his art.

"Can I ask you something?" she said.

"Yeah."

"How long have you been making this series?"

"Since the beginning of the year." He looked at the photographs. "I've been looking for people who have that quality, the full presence quality. It's rare. Most people, even here, are making posed work even when they think they're not." He looked back at her. "You're not."

She thought about Mr. Osei.

"Posed work shows you how people want to be seen," she said. "Captured moments show you who they actually are."

He looked at her. "I said that to you in the hallway."

"You did."

"You remembered it."

"I remember things that are true," she said simply.

They stood in the red light of the darkroom looking at his series and her panels and the specific intersection of their two bodies of work.

The intersection felt significant.

She was not going to say that out loud.

But she felt it.

"These are honest," she said finally. About the series.

He looked at her like that was exactly what he had needed to hear.

"I wasn't sure," he said. "If they were good."

"They're not safe," she said.

"No." He almost smiled. "They're really not."

"That's how you know," she said.

He nodded slowly.

They walked out of the darkroom together into the bright ordinary hallway and the sounds of the building came back and the school day reasserted itself around them and nothing was the same as it had been before she followed him through that door.

Not dramatically different.

Just shifted.

The way things shifted when someone saw you clearly and you let yourself know it.

He put me in his art.
Not as a background.
As the subject.
He found something in my panels worth capturing.
He found something in me worth capturing.
I do not know what to do with that
except to keep making honest work
and see what happens next.
Post the uncertain work.
Always.

She called Simone that evening.

Not texted. Called. Because what had happened in the darkroom was not a text conversation.

Simone answered on the second ring.

"He put my work in his series," Nova said without preamble.

A pause.

"Tell me everything," Simone said.

So she told her. All of it. The darkroom and the red light and the twenty photographs and the fourteenth one, her panels breathing in his photograph, catching light. What he had said about full presence.

What she had said about true things. The moment before they walked out.

Simone listened without interrupting until Nova finished.

"He put you in his art," Simone said.

"He put my panels"

"He put you in his art," Simone said again, more firmly. "Nova. He looked at what you made and he saw you in it and he thought you were worth documenting." A pause. "He likes you."

"We don't know"

"We absolutely know," Simone said. "Nova. He put you in his art."

Nova looked at the ceiling of her pink bedroom.

"That could just be artistic appreciation," she said.

"It is artistic appreciation," Simone said. "And it is also him liking you. Both things. At the same time. That is how it works when it is real."

Nova drew a small spiral in the margin of her sketchbook.

"What do I do?"

"Nothing," Simone said. "You keep being you. You let it develop. You don't perform anything. You just keep being Nova and see what happens."

Nova thought about that.

"That's good advice."

"I know," Simone said. "You've been a good teacher."

Nova smiled at the ceiling.

"I have," she agreed.

She Rose — Reflection

- Has anyone ever seen you so clearly that you felt it as something physical, as warmth, as recognition, as the specific relief of being known?
- What is the difference between someone admiring you and someone truly seeing you? Which one have you experienced more?
- What would it mean to stop hiding the uncertain work and let yourself be seen as you actually are?
- Who in your life is paying close enough attention to put you in their art, their story, their work, their life?

> *I am worth seeing. All of me. The uncertain working version. The still-figuring-it-out version. The version that makes things in the dark and does not know if they are good until they are done. That version is worth the frame. I let myself be seen. Starting now.*

She Rose

He put her in his art. Not because she was finished or perfect or safe. Because she was present. Because the uncertain work she had almost not posted had something real in it that his eye could not walk past. Post the uncertain work. Always.

CHAPTER 6

What Going Viral Actually Feels Like

I posted at eleven PM.
I was too tired to second guess myself.
That was the whole strategy.
Wait until you are too tired to be afraid.
Then post.
I went to sleep.
I woke up to forty thousand notifications.
My phone was warm from the activity.
Like it had been working all night while I slept.
Like the world had found something
while I was not watching.
I do not know how to feel about this yet.
I am going to figure it out.
Right after I figure out why my hands are shaking.

The piece had been made on a Wednesday evening in late November.

Not planned. Not scheduled. Not the result of a deliberate creative session where she had sat down with the intention of making something significant. It had arrived the way the best things always arrived: out of nowhere, from the part of her brain that worked on things without her conscious permission, presenting itself fully formed in the middle of something else entirely.

She had been doing homework.

Math. The specific focused tedium of a problem set. She had been aware of the parallel process for about twenty minutes before she acknowledged it. The image that was forming in the background. Not a panel. Not a sequential piece. Something she had never made before: a single full-page spread that was simultaneously representational and abstract, figurative and geometric, manga-influenced and something else entirely. Something that was all of her influences in conversation with each other rather than any single one of them in isolation.

She closed the math homework.

She opened her sketchbook.

She drew for three hours without stopping.

Not with the deliberate application of Mr. Osei's rules, though the rules were operating in the background as they always operated now. This was beyond the rules. This was the place that the rules had been preparing her for: the place on the other side of the certain where the real voice lived. She had been building toward this place since September.

She arrived there on a Wednesday night doing math homework.

When she looked up from the page three hours later the room was dark except for her desk lamp and the drawing in front of her was the best thing she had ever made.

She knew it immediately. Not with arrogance. With the specific clarity of someone who had made enough things to know the difference between good and extraordinary.

This was the second kind.

She photographed it.

She held her phone.

She looked at the image on her screen for a long time.

Post the uncertain work.

She was not uncertain about this piece. She was certain it was good. But she was uncertain about what it was, what category it fit in, whether the departure from her established style would be received as growth.

That uncertainty was enough.

She posted it at eleven PM when she was too tired to let the uncertainty become an obstacle.

No caption.

Just the image.

She went to sleep.

She woke up to forty thousand notifications.

Not forty. Not four hundred. Not four thousand.

Forty thousand.

Her phone had been charging on her nightstand and when her alarm went off she reached for it and the screen was lit with a density of activity she had never seen before. The notification center was full and still updating in real time as she watched it. Likes. Comments. Follows. Shares. Reposts. Tags. The specific cascading activity of something that had been passed from person to person through the night while she slept.

She sat up.

She stared at her phone.

Her follower count had been four thousand, two hundred when she went to sleep.

It was now ten thousand, six hundred and forty-one.

She read the number three times.

Then she put her phone face down on the bed and sat in the quiet of her bedroom for a full minute trying to locate herself. Her pink room. Her sketchbooks on the shelf. The drawing on her desk, the original, the physical object, the paper and pencil marks that had been the source of all of this overnight activity.

She was still Nova Cole.

She was still fifteen.

She was still in the middle of freshman year at Westbrook Academy for the Arts.

All of that was still true.

She picked up her phone.

She opened the post.

The comments were extraordinary.

I have been looking at this for fifteen minutes and I still see something new every time. The line work in the upper left quadrant: I've never seen anything do what this does. This is the first piece of art that has made me cry in years. Who IS this? I study sequential art at university and this is more sophisticated than most work I see from my peers.

She read them slowly.

All of them.

She let each one land before she moved to the next because they deserved that.

She was three-quarters of the way through the comments when she found the others.

There were not many of them. In the ratio of thousands of comments they were a small fraction.

Why does she always make it about being different. The neurodivergent artist aesthetic is so overdone right now. The stimming references in the line work are so forced. We get it.

Nova stopped scrolling.

She read those three comments again.

Then she put her phone down on her desk and looked at the drawing.

The original. The physical piece. The thing that had come out of three hours of uninterrupted making on a Wednesday night when she was too tired to manage the output.

She looked at it for a long time.

The stimming references in the line work.

She had not consciously put stimming references in the line work.

Or had she?

She leaned closer.

The lines in the lower right section, the ones that had come in the second hour when she had stopped thinking entirely and her hands had moved into pure automaticity, did have a pattern. A specific repeating quality. The rhythm of them.

She recognized it.

It was the pattern her hands made.

Her specific pattern. The one her body had developed over years of self-regulation. The small movement that her fingers did when her nervous system needed to process something at a volume that exceeded the ordinary.

She had drawn herself into the work.

Without knowing she was doing it.

And someone had seen it.

And called it forced.

She sat with her hands in her lap.

Her foot began its tap against the floor. Automatic. Her body taking care of itself the way it always had, without her permission, without her management, without caring whether anyone in the room found it inconvenient or overdone.

She looked at her tapping foot.

She thought about sixth grade. About the hallway and Kayla and the word weird landing in her chest like something cold. About the three months of holding the stim. About the specific cost of that.

I will not let anyone make me feel any other way than who I am.

She had said that back to her mother three times in sixth grade.

She picked up her phone.

She opened the comments again.

She found the three negative ones.

She read them one more time.

And then she scrolled past them.

All the way past them.

Back to the thousands of others.

Back to I have been looking at this for fifteen minutes.

Back to This is the first piece of art that has made me cry in years.

She put her phone down.

She picked up her pencil.

She wrote in her sketchbook.

Someone said my neurodivergence was forced.
My neurodivergence is not forced.
It is the most unforced thing about me.
It is in my hands when I draw.
It is in my feet when they tap.
It is in my eyes when they find compositions
that other people walk past without seeing.
It is in my brain that processes everything
at a volume that has sometimes been overwhelming
and has also been the source of every honest piece of work
I have ever made.
My neurodivergence is not a reference.
It is not an aesthetic.
It is not a choice.
It is me.
I am not going to apologize for that.
Not now.

Not ever.
Not again.

She showed Marcus the comments the next day.

She had not planned to. She just did, the natural result of being in a conversation with someone she trusted and having the thing be present enough in her mind that it found its way into the conversation without being summoned.

They were in the courtyard at lunch.

She handed him her phone. He read without saying anything for a moment. Then he handed the phone back.

"The people who said that," he said carefully, "are people who have never made anything uncertain. People who make safe work always criticize the work that isn't safe. Because it makes them uncomfortable." He looked at her. "Your neurodivergence is in your work. That's not a flaw. That's your signature. That's the thing that makes your line work recognizable from across a room."

Nova looked at him.

"You can see it?"

"Everyone who knows how to look can see it," he said. "It's beautiful, Nova."

She felt the words land.

Not just about the art.

All the way in.

She Rose — Reflection

◆ What is the thing about you, your specific way of being in the world, your particular kind of different, that someone has tried to make you feel should be hidden or minimized?

◆ What would it mean to put that thing into your work instead? To let it be the signature rather than the flaw?

◆ When something you made or said or did reached people who needed it, what did that feel like? How did it change how you thought about sharing your work?

◆ Who in your life sees clearly enough to say: that thing that makes you different is beautiful? Do you let yourself receive it when they say it?

> *I do not apologize for who I am. Not in my work. Not in my life. Not for anyone. The things that make me different are not liabilities. They are qualifications. They are my signature. They are the most honest thing about me. And I am proud of every single one.*

She Rose

She drew herself into the work without knowing. Because that is what happens when you make uncertain work. You show up in it. All of you. The parts you chose and the parts you were born with. And the right people will recognize you in it and it will be the most important thing.

CHAPTER 7

The Girl Who Became a Mirror

Jordan came to find me today.
Not to compete.
Not to assess.
Just to show me something.
She sat down across from me
and opened her sketchbook
and said can I show you something
in a voice I had never heard from her before.
Stripped of the competitive edge.
Just a person's voice.
Just a girl who needed another girl to look at something honestly.
I looked.
I told her the truth.
Something shifted between us.
I think rivals are sometimes just friends
who have not found the right door yet.

The January light at Westbrook was different from the September light.

Nova had noticed this gradually over the first semester, the way the quality of illumination in the building changed with the season, the north-facing windows that had poured warm late-summer light across the studio tables in September now delivering something cooler and more horizontal, the sun lower in the sky, the shadows longer.

She had drawn the light three times in her sketchbook. Not as a subject, as a study. The way light changed was the way time passed and she wanted to document it.

She was doing this on a Tuesday afternoon in the second week of January, sitting at her usual spot by the north windows, sketchbook open to a study of the light pattern falling across the empty easels on the far wall, when Jordan sat down across from her.

Not at the far end of the table.

Across from her.

The specific proximate choice of someone who had decided on closeness rather than distance.

Nova looked up.

Jordan had her own sketchbook in her hands. She was holding it the way people held things they were uncertain about, not loosely but with a slight tension in the grip.

"Can I show you something?" she said.

Her voice was different.

Nova had been listening to Jordan's voice for four months across a worktable and she knew its registers. The competitive one, precise, slightly clipped. The social one, warmer, the competitive edge softened.

This was something underneath both of those.

"Yeah," Nova said.

Jordan opened the sketchbook.

The work inside was not what Nova had expected.

She had seen Jordan's work extensively by this point, the manga panels in the entrance, the pieces she posted online, the projects she brought to the seminar. She knew Jordan's hand.

This was not that work.

These pages were loose. Personal. The line quality was different, not because Jordan's technical skill had deteriorated but because it had been deliberately set aside, the precision traded for something more immediate. The drawings were autobiographical in a way that was unmistakable once you knew what you were looking at.

Raw. That was the word.

The specific rawness of work made without protection.

Nova looked at the pages slowly. Really looked. Not page by page in isolation but as a sequence, the accumulation of images building toward something she could feel but not yet fully articulate.

When she looked up Jordan was watching her with an expression she recognized.

The specific vulnerability of someone who had shown something real and was waiting to find out if the showing had been a mistake.

"Nothing is wrong with it," Nova said.

Jordan exhaled.

"It doesn't look like my work."

"I know." Nova looked back at the pages. "That's why it's good."

Jordan looked at her.

"Mr. Osei said"

"Make something uncertain," Nova said.

"Yeah."

"He said that to me too. First seminar."

"What did you do with it?"

Nova thought about the three panels on the board. The non-dominant hand drawing. The dark drawing. The continuous line. The viral post. All of it, the whole chain of consequence that had followed from the decision to stop making safe work.

"I made something in the dark," she said. "Literally. I turned the light off and drew for ten minutes and then turned it on."

Jordan looked at her. "That's where the texture came from. In the piece you posted."

"Yeah."

"I spent an hour trying to figure out how you did that."

Nova looked at her. "So did I. On your panel transitions. In October."

Jordan blinked. "You studied my transitions?"

"For forty minutes." Nova paused. "Right after I spent forty-five minutes comparing our follower counts."

The silence that followed was not awkward.

It was the specific silence of two people recognizing themselves in each other's confession.

Jordan laughed first.

Not the careful social laugh. The real one, surprised out of her, genuine.

"I did the same thing," she said. "With your count. In October."

"We were both doing that?"

"Apparently."

Nova shook her head slowly. "We wasted so much time."

"We really did," Jordan said.

They looked at each other across the worktable. Four months of careful assessment and competitive watchfulness and mutual respect that had never quite found the door into something warmer.

The door was open now.

"Can I give you one note?" Nova said. About the sketchbook pages.

"Please," Jordan said.

"The transition between page three and page four." Nova turned to it. "You're rushing it. You're right here," she pointed to a specific image, "and this is where the emotional truth of the sequence is. Everything before it has been building to this moment. And then you move past it too quickly." She looked up. "Stay in it longer. Let it be as uncomfortable as it actually is. The discomfort is the whole point of this page."

Jordan looked at the image.

She was quiet for a moment.

"That's exactly what I've been avoiding," she said quietly.

"I know," Nova said. "I could see it."

"How?"

Nova thought about it.

"Because I do the same thing in my work," she said. "When something is too true I move past it faster than I should. Mr. Osei calls it rushing the landing." She paused. "The reader needs time to land in the emotional truth before you move them forward. If you rush them they don't feel it."

Jordan looked at the page for a long time.

"You sound like him," she said.

"He's in my head," Nova said. "All the time. Constantly."

Jordan smiled. "Mine too."

She closed the sketchbook.

She looked at Nova with an expression that had none of the competitive assessment in it. Just a person looking at another person. With something like relief.

"I think we could have been friends from the beginning," she said.

"I think so too," Nova said. "We're going to be really annoying to be around together."

"Why?"

"Because we're both going to push each other." Nova said it like a fact. "Neither of us is going to let the other make safe work. We're going to call it out every time."

Jordan considered this.

"That sounds terrible," she said.

"I know," Nova agreed.

"I want that," Jordan said.

"Me too," Nova said.

They looked at each other.

Two girls who had been rivals for four months finding out they had always been something else.

"I'm going to redo pages three and four," Jordan said. "Tonight."

"Good," Nova said.

"I'm not going to like it."

"No," Nova agreed. "But you'll know it's right."

Jordan stood up. She tucked her sketchbook under her arm, less tension in the grip now.

"Nova," she said.

"Yeah."

"Thank you."

"Thank you for sitting across from me," Nova said. "Specifically. Not at the end of the table."

Jordan smiled. The real one.

And walked away.

Nova turned back to her light study.

She looked at the January light on the empty easels.

She picked up her pencil.

She wrote in the margin of the page:

She was never my enemy. She was just the mirror I needed. The friction that makes you sharper. The people who challenge us most are sometimes the people who love us best. I think Jordan is going to be one of those people. I think she already is.

She Rose — Reflection

- ◆ Is there someone in your life you have been treating as a rival when they might actually be a mirror? What would happen if you sat across from them instead of at the end of the table?
- ◆ What does the work you make when nobody is watching look like? Does it look like your public work or like something different? What does the difference tell you?
- ◆ Who in your life calls you to do your best work, not by praising everything you make but by telling you the truth about it?
- ◆ What is the thing you have been rushing past in your own work, your own relationships, your own life, because sitting with it is uncomfortable?

> *The people who challenge me are not my enemies. They are my growth. I welcome the friction. I welcome the mirror. I am not threatened by someone else's excellence. I am made sharper by it. And I am generous enough to offer the same. That is what real community looks like. I choose it.*

She Rose

She was never my enemy. She was just the mirror I needed. The friction that makes you sharper. The rivalry that was always going to become the friendship. The door that was always there waiting for the right moment to open.

CHAPTER 8

The Mentor's Question

Mr. Osei called me in today.
Not for a critique.
Not for feedback on a specific piece.
Just a conversation.
He had all of my work from the semester
spread across the large table in his office.
All of it.
September through February.
The whole arc.
I had not seen it laid out like that before.
All in one place.
All in sequence.
I looked at it for a long time.
I could see myself in it.
Not in the way you see yourself in a photograph.
In the way you see yourself in the record of a year.
In the evidence of who you were becoming
while you were too busy becoming to notice.

Mr. Osei's office was small and exactly what you would expect from a working artist who also happened to occupy an institutional space.

The desk was functional rather than impressive: a large worktable covered in the controlled disorder of someone who worked in multiple things simultaneously and had developed a personal system for navigating that disorder that would be incomprehensible to anyone else. Reference images pinned to the wall behind it. Books stacked horizontally on top of other books on shelves that had long since exceeded their intended capacity. A print in a simple frame, a page from a graphic novel Nova did not recognize, a single panel, a figure standing at the edge of something with their back to the viewer, the space before them completely open.

She had looked at that print every time she had been in the office.

She had never asked about it.

Today she was going to ask.

"Who made that?" she said when she sat down.

Mr. Osei turned to look at the print. He was quiet for a moment, the specific quiet of someone whose relationship with a thing went deep enough that the question required actual thought.

"A student," he said finally. "From fifteen years ago."

Nova looked at the figure in the panel. The open space ahead of them. The specific quality of the image: a figure poised at the beginning of something without knowing what it was.

"It's extraordinary," she said.

"Yes," he said simply. "She was."

He turned to the table where Nova's work was spread.

"Look at this," he said. Not as an instruction. As an invitation.

Nova looked.

She had seen each piece individually as she made it. Had lived with each one. She had seen the pieces in the seminar room during critiques. She had not seen them together like this.

All of them. September through February. Laid out in chronological sequence across the large worktable so that the arc was visible: the shape of a year of work, the evidence of growth not just in individual pieces but in the movement between them.

The September work was technically accomplished. She had known that then and she knew it now. The clean line work, the sophisticated panel composition. It was good work. It was the best work she had been capable of making in September.

It was also clearly the work of someone who knew what they were doing and was doing it.

The October work was different.

She could see the shift clearly from this distance: the place where the rules had begun to operate, where the comfort had started giving way to something less certain and more alive.

The viral piece was in the center of the spread. It was physically larger than most of the other pieces. Looking at it surrounded by the work that had preceded it she could see exactly what it was. Not a departure. An arrival. The place where everything that had come before had been pointing.

And the January and February work had a quality she had not been able to name when she was inside them. She could name it now.

Freedom.

Not the absence of discipline. The presence of a specific creative freedom that came from having done enough uncertain work to stop being afraid of the uncertainty.

She looked at the spread for a long time.

"Do you know what happened here?" Mr. Osei said.

"I got less safe," she said.

"Yes," he said. "And?"

She kept looking at the work.

"I showed up more," she said. "In the work. I stopped keeping myself separate from it."

"Yes," he said. "And do you know why that happened?"

She thought about it honestly.

"Because I stopped protecting myself from the work," she said slowly. "I stopped being afraid of what would happen if the work was really about me. If it had my specific brain and my specific hands and my specific way of seeing in it rather than the version of those things that

I thought was acceptable." She paused. "The uncertain work let me do that."

Mr. Osei looked at her for a moment.

"I have a question for you," he said. "And I want you to think before you answer."

"Okay."

"What do you want to do with this?" He gestured at the spread. The whole year. "Not what do you think you should do. Not what would be impressive. What do you actually want?"

The question settled into the room.

Nova looked at the work.

She thought about sixth grade. About the sketchbook in the bag and the sketchbook in her hand and the three years of work between those two moments. About the regional showcase and the second place ribbon and Nana Rose saying you made your story. About the entrance hallway at Westbrook and the manga panels and Jordan across the table. About the darkroom and Marcus and forty thousand notifications and the comment that had tried to make her neurodivergence something to apologize for.

About the morning ritual. About I walk like I have ten thousand ancestors protecting me.

About why she made things at all.

"I want to tell stories," she said. "True ones. The kind that make people feel less alone. The kind that could only have been made by me, by my specific brain and my specific hands and my specific way of seeing the world." She paused. "I want to be the kind of artist whose work you recognize from across a room. Not because it follows a recognizable style. Because it has a recognizable truth in it."

She had not planned to say the next part.

But it was true. And true things found their way out when you were in the right room with the right person asking the right question.

"And I want to make things that reach the girls who are like me. The neurodivergent ones. The ones who have been told their way of being in the world is something to manage rather than something to make from. I want to make work that says: this is what your brain looks like when it makes something. And it's extraordinary."

Mr. Osei was quiet.

Then he reached into the folder on his desk and placed a document on the table.

"The Young Artists National Showcase," he said. "Deadline is April. Submit the viral piece and the six strongest pieces from the second half of the semester." He looked at her steadily. "This work is ready."

Nova looked at the document.

"The National Showcase."

"Yes."

"I'm a freshman."

"I'm aware."

"Nobody submits as a freshman."

"You are not nobody," he said. "Submit the work."

She looked at the spread one more time. At the whole year laid out. At the record of a girl becoming an artist.

"Okay," she said.

"Okay?"

"I'll submit."

Mr. Osei nodded once. The specific nod of someone who had always known this was going to be the answer and was simply waiting for her to know it too.

She stood up to leave.

"Nova," he said.

She turned.

He was looking at the print on the wall. The figure at the edge of the open space. The beginning of something unnamed.

"The student who made that," he said. "She was also fifteen when I first told her to submit work she was not sure was ready." He looked back at Nova. "She was wrong about it not being ready. So are you."

Nova looked at the print.

At the figure standing at the edge of everything.

She understood now what she had always been looking at.

Not a figure looking out at an unknown future.

A figure who had just arrived at the beginning of something real.

"Thank you," she said.

She walked out of the office carrying the application in her hand.

He wants me to submit to the National Showcase.
I am going to submit to the National Showcase.
The youngest person ever accepted was sixteen.
I am fifteen.
I am submitting anyway.
Not because I think I will get in.
Because the work is ready.
Because Mr. Osei said so.
Because I have learned to trust the people who see me clearly.
Reina taught me that.
Nana Rose taught me that.
Ms. Carter taught me that.
Mr. Osei is teaching me that.
Submit the work.
Whatever happens after is what happens after.
But submit the work.
Always.

Submit.

She Rose — Reflection

◆ If someone laid out the full record of your year, every choice, every piece of work, every decision about who you were going to be in each moment, what would the arc look like? Are you getting less safe or more?

◆ What do you actually want? Not what you think you should want. Not what would look good to other people. What do you want, honestly, from the inside?

◆ Who is the Mr. Osei in your life, the person who sees you clearly enough to push you past what you think your limits are?

◆ What is the application you have been afraid to submit, the thing you have been waiting to be more ready for before you try?

> *I know what I want. I am allowed to want it. I am allowed to say it out loud. Even the parts I did not plan to say. Especially those parts. The unplanned truth is always the most important one. I speak it. I claim it. I submit the work.*

She Rose

You are not nobody. Submit the work. Whatever happens after is what happens after. But submit the work. You cannot receive what you never reach for.

CHAPTER 9

What Heartbreak Teaches You

I know what I saw.
I am not going to perform not having seen it.
I saw it.
It landed in my chest the way true things land.
Quietly.
Completely.
Without asking permission.
The question is not whether it hurt.
It did.
The question is what I am going to do
with the hurting.
I already know the answer.
I am going to feel it fully.
And I am not going to shrink.
Not once.
Not for this.
Not for anyone.

The thing about caring about someone was that it happened gradually and then completely.

Nova had been aware of Marcus for months before she understood what that awareness was. Had looked forward to the hallway moments and the courtyard lunches and the specific quality of being in a conversation where both people were fully present without identifying what the looking forward was made of. Had felt the warmth in the darkroom and the specific something of being put in his art and had let Simone tell her what it meant without fully letting herself know it.

And then at some point, not a specific moment, more like a gradual settling into clarity, she had known.

She cared about him.

In the specific way that fifteen felt things: completely, without the self-protective moderation that came with experience, with the full unguarded openness of someone who had not yet been through enough heartbreak to build the appropriate defenses against it.

She had let herself know it.

And she had let herself act from it, not dramatically, not with a declaration or a performance. Just the natural expression of it. The increased time together. The conversations that went deeper. The specific ease of being with someone who spoke your language and saw your work and asked the real questions.

It had been good.

And then it had shifted.

She noticed the shift the way she noticed everything: before she could name it, in the accumulation of small observations that her brain processed and filed before her conscious mind had caught up.

The texts taking slightly longer to be answered. Not by much, but a margin that Nova registered.

The courtyard lunches happening less frequently.

The quality of his presence in conversation, still warm, still real, but with a slight distance in it that had not been there before.

She noticed all of it.

She told herself she was reading too much into it.

She told herself this story three times a day for two weeks.

On the day she walked past the darkroom and saw Marcus inside, showing his work to a girl from the senior class, saw his face in profile through the small window in the door with the quality of attention directed at someone else in the way it had once been directed at her, she stopped telling herself the story.

She kept walking.

She went to the studio.

She sat at her worktable.

She opened her sketchbook to a fresh page.

She did not draw anything.

She sat with the blank page and the specific feeling of something she had allowed herself to care about shifting in a direction she had not chosen and could not control.

She let the feeling exist.

She did not push it down.

She did not rush to resolve it.

She sat with it the way she sat with difficult work, with patience, with honest attention, without demanding that it become something more manageable than it actually was.

It hurt.

She let it hurt.

That was new.

She talked to Reina that night.

Not immediately. She needed the afternoon first. Time for the feeling to settle into something she could speak accurately. Time to separate the part that was grief from the part that was humiliation and the part that was disappointment and the part that was the specific hurt of caring about someone who was caring about someone else.

She found her mother in the kitchen after dinner.

The specific kitchen comfort of her childhood: the smells and the light and the familiar geography of a space that had held a thousand important conversations. Her mother at the counter. The particular quality of Reina's presence in the room, warm and steady and fully available in the way she became available when she sensed that her daughter needed something real.

"Mom," Nova said.

Reina turned.

She looked at her daughter's face with the full reading attention of a woman who had been studying this specific face for fifteen years.

"Tell me," she said.

Nova told her.

All of it. Marcus and the months of accumulation and the specific warmth of it and the gradual shift and the story she had been telling herself and the day she had stopped telling it. The darkroom window and what she had seen and what it had felt like and the blank sketchbook page in the studio afterward.

Reina listened.

She did not interrupt. She did not finish sentences. She did not rush toward the part where Nova felt better. Just listened, with the specific quality of listening that Nova had needed her whole life and had been given her whole life and only now understood was not something every person received.

"How do you feel right now?" Reina said when Nova finished. "Not about him. About yourself."

Nova thought about it.

"Sad," she said. "But clear. Like I saw something true and I didn't pretend I didn't."

Reina looked at her steadily.

"That's different from sixth grade," she said.

"I know."

"In sixth grade you pushed things down."

"I know."

"You held the stim in the hallway. You left the sketchbook in the bag. You adjusted and managed and performed being okay for months."

"I know."

"You're not doing that now."

"No," Nova said. "It hurts but I'm not pushing it down."

Reina was quiet for a moment.

"Can I tell you something?"

"Yeah."

"Heartbreak teaches you things that nothing else can," she said. "Not because the pain is good, it's not. But because the way you move through it tells you exactly who you are and exactly what you will and will not accept." She looked at Nova directly. "The fact that you saw what you saw and you are not pretending you didn't, that you are sitting here feeling it instead of managing it, that is not small. That took me years to learn."

Nova looked at her mother.

She thought about the hospital bed. About the phone call. About the years of patient loving that had cost Reina everything. About the woman who had finally stopped pushing things down and built her life from the truth instead.

"I learned from watching you," Nova said quietly.

Reina was still.

"You learned from watching me get it wrong," she said.

"I learned from watching you get it right eventually," Nova said. "That matters too."

Reina opened her arms.

Nova walked into them.

The conversation with Marcus was brief and kind.

She had initiated it, not because she owed him an accounting but because she had things to say and saying them was part of moving through it honestly rather than around it.

"I think I got scared," he said. "Of how real it was getting. That's not an excuse. I just want you to know it wasn't about you."

"I know," Nova said. And meant it.

"I still think your work is extraordinary," he said.

"I know that too," she said. "It always was. It'll keep being."

She walked away from that conversation feeling something she had not expected to feel.

Whole.

Not healed. Not over it. It still hurt in the specific way that first heartbreaks hurt: the grief of possibility rather than loss, the mourning of something that could have been rather than something that was. But whole. Like herself. Like someone who had moved through something without losing any part of herself in it.

Not diminished. Not adjusted. Not smaller.

She went home that evening and sat at her desk.

She opened her sketchbook.

She drew for two hours.

Not processing the heartbreak. Not working through the feeling on the page the way she sometimes did. Just drawing, because drawing was what she did, because the sketchbook was in her hand where it belonged, because the practice did not stop for heartbreak.

The work she made that evening was some of the best of the year.

Not in spite of what had happened.

Because she had moved through it as herself.

I did not shrink.

Not once.
That is the whole lesson.
That is everything.

She Rose — Reflection

◆ Think about a time you were hurt by someone you cared about. Did you feel it fully or did you push it down? What did pushing it down cost you?

◆ What does it mean to move through something as yourself, without shrinking, without adjusting, without leaving pieces of yourself behind in the experience?

◆ What is the heartbreak that taught you the most important thing you know about your own worth?

◆ How do you know when you have moved through something with your whole self intact?

> *I feel things fully. I do not push them down. I do not perform okay before I actually am okay. I move through hard things as myself. Completely. Without shrinking. Without adjusting. Without leaving any part of myself behind. I come out the other side whole. I always do. Because I am made of things that do not break.*

She Rose

I did not shrink. Not once. That is the whole lesson. The measure of who you are is not whether hard things happen to you. It is who you are when you come out the other side. Come out whole. Every time.

CHAPTER 10

She Rose

The letter from the National Showcase arrived on a Friday in June.

The last week of freshman year. The hallways of Westbrook had the particular energy of endings: the bittersweet warmth of a year that had been full and difficult and transformative arriving at its natural conclusion. Students clearing their lockers. Final critiques completed. The walls of the student work board in the main hallway being cleared to make space for the next year's work.

Nova was in the studio when Mr. Osei found her.

He had the letter in his hand.

She looked at his face and knew before he said anything.

"You got in," he said.

I got in.
The National Showcase.
Fifteen years old.
Freshman year.
I got in.
I don't have words yet.
I'm going to draw it.
Same as always.
Same as it has always been.
When the feeling is too big for words
it goes in the sketchbook.
My sketchbook.
The one I almost stopped carrying.
The one I carry in my hand now.
Always.
In my hand.
Where it belongs.

Jordan found out at the same time. She had submitted too, had told Nova quietly in April without making a production of it, and they had not discussed it since in the unspoken agreement of two people who were too invested in the outcome to speak it out loud.

Jordan got in too.

They found out within minutes of each other and met in the hallway outside the studio and stood there looking at each other.

"We both got in," Jordan said.

"We both got in," Nova confirmed.

They looked at each other for a moment.

And then Jordan, precise controlled composed Jordan who had spent the entire year maintaining the careful edge of competition, laughed. Full and genuine and completely undone.

Nova laughed too.

They stood in the hallway of Westbrook Academy for the Arts on the last Friday of freshman year and laughed together like they had been doing it for years.

Maybe they had been.

Maybe they had just been laughing in parallel until they figured out how to do it together.

That evening Nova sat on the floor of her bedroom.

Not her old pink bedroom. A different room in the same suburb, still pink because of course it was still pink, but also with a dedicated drawing wall now where she pinned work in progress and reference images and things that inspired her. A room that looked like a studio and also looked like her.

She had her sketchbook in her lap.

She opened it to the first page of the year. September. The day she had arrived at Westbrook.

I got in. I am still not sure I believe it. I got in on my manga. The thing I almost stopped doing in sixth grade.

She read it.

She thought about the year. All of it.

The thirty-foot ceiling and the manga panels on the wall. Jordan across the worktable with her competitive eyes. Mr. Osei and the word safe and the rule that had changed everything. The uncertain panels posted on the board in the hallway. Marcus stopping to look. The dark drawing and the viral post and the comment that had tried to make her neurodivergence something to apologize for. Jordan's uncertain pages and the note that had turned a rival into a friend. The National Showcase letter.

And Marcus. And the heartbreak. And the thing it had taught her.

I did not shrink.

She closed the first sketchbook of the year.

She opened a new one.

She wrote on the first page:

Sophomore year. Nova Cole. Artist. National Showcase. Here we go.

She put the pen down.

She went to her mirror.

Her locs fell over her shoulders. Her honey brown eyes were steady. The girl in the reflection was fifteen years old and had just completed the most significant year of her life so far and was standing on the other side of it: not unscathed, not unchanged, but whole. Completely, undeniably, fiercely whole.

She put her hand on her heart.

She said the words.

The ones she had been saying since she was old enough to stand at a mirror with her mother. The ones that had sometimes been rushed and sometimes been slow and had always, even in the rushed versions, even in the seasons when she had forgotten what they meant, been true.

I love myself.

I am more than enough.

Today is going to be an amazing day.

I am intelligent. I am strong. I am powerful.

Everything I need is already inside me.

I am a goddess.

I walk like I have ten thousand ancestors protecting me.

She looked at the girl in the mirror.

At the artist who had gotten into the National Showcase at fifteen.

At the girl who had moved through heartbreak without shrinking.

At the neurodivergent girl who had drawn herself into her work without knowing and then refused to apologize for it.

At the girl who had arrived at this school carrying a sketchbook in her hand and had never put it in her bag.

Not once.

Not this year.

She smiled.

The real smile.

There she is, she said softly.

There she was.

Nova Cole.

Fifteen years old.

Rising.

She Rose — Reflection

- ◆ What is the most important thing you learned about yourself this year? Not from a test. From your life.
- ◆ What is the new story you are about to start, the next chapter, the next school year, the next version of your life, and what do you want to carry into it?
- ◆ What would you write on the first page of your next sketchbook?
- ◆ Say the whole morning ritual out loud right now. Every word. Slowly. Meaning all of it.

> *I love myself. I am more than enough. Today is going to be an amazing day. I am intelligent. I am strong. I am powerful. Everything I need is already inside me. I am a goddess. I walk like I have ten thousand ancestors protecting me. And I will never stop rising.*

She Rose

She rose. Not because the year was easy. Because she showed up for it as herself, completely, consistently, without putting her sketchbook in her bag. Not once. Not this year. Carry yours in your hand. Always. Where it belongs.

A NOTE FROM THE AUTHOR

Nova got into Westbrook on the work she almost stopped making.

She got into the National Showcase on the work she was not sure about.

She moved through heartbreak without losing herself.

She turned a rival into a friend.

She posted the uncertain work.

She is fifteen.

She is just beginning.

I wrote this book for every girl who is standing where Nova is standing: at the beginning of something big, something uncertain, something that is going to require all of you.

Not the safe version.

Not the edited version.

Not the version that keeps the sketchbook in the bag.

All of you.

Your neurodivergence is not a flaw.

Your sensitivity is not a weakness.

Your art, whatever your art is, is not something to hide.

Carry it in your hand.

Where it belongs.

With love,

Kendra Tamika

ACKNOWLEDGEMENTS

This book would not exist without the people who held me and the people who inspired me.

To my daughter: you are Nova. You have always been Nova. Thank you for being exactly who you are every single day without apology. Watching you navigate this world with joy and courage and complete authenticity is the greatest gift of my life.

To my mother: thank you for being Nana Rose. For the wisdom you passed down. For the sentences that became the spine of this entire series.

To my little sisters and every young woman in my life: this series is for you. I wrote it so you would have something to hold in your hands on the days when the world tries to make you forget. You were born knowing. Never let anyone convince you otherwise.

To every neurodivergent girl who has ever been made to feel like the way her body works is something to hide: Nova is for you specifically. Your stimming is not a flaw. It is your body taking care of itself. Honor it.

And to every girl who picks up this book in her hardest season:

You are seen.

You are enough.

You are that girl.

Now go remember her.

Also by Kendra Tamika:

Remember Her

The moment a woman stops searching for power and realizes she already is it.

She Always Knew — For the girl ages 6 to 9

She Remembered — For the girl ages 10 to 13

She Arrived — For the young woman ages 18 to 25

www.ingramcontent.com/pod-product-compliance
Lightning Source LLC
La Vergne TN
LVHW010832120826
845149LV00016B/978
9798995470564